TOMIE dePAOLA

My Mother Is So Smart!

G. P. Putnam's Sons · An Imprint of Penguin Group (USA) Inc.

For my mother, Flossie,
and all the other smart mothers
in the world

G. P. PUTNAM'S SONS
A division of Penguin Young Readers Group.
Published by The Penguin Group.
Penguin Group (USA) Inc., 375 Hudson Street, New York, NY 10014, U.S.A.
Penguin Group (Canada), 90 Eglinton Avenue East, Suite 700, Toronto, Ontario M4P 2Y3, Canada
(a division of Pearson Penguin Canada Inc.).
Penguin Books Ltd, 80 Strand, London WC2R 0RL, England.
Penguin Ireland, 25 St. Stephen's Green, Dublin 2, Ireland (a division of Penguin Books Ltd.).
Penguin Group (Australia), 250 Camberwell Road, Camberwell, Victoria 3124, Australia
(a division of Pearson Australia Group Pty Ltd).
Penguin Books India Pvt Ltd, 11 Community Centre, Panchsheel Park, New Delhi - 110 017, India.
Penguin Group (NZ), 67 Apollo Drive, Rosedale, North Shore 0632, New Zealand (a division of Pearson New Zealand Ltd).
Penguin Books (South Africa) (Pty) Ltd, 24 Sturdee Avenue, Rosebank, Johannesburg 2196, South Africa.
Penguin Books Ltd, Registered Offices: 80 Strand, London WC2R 0RL, England.

Library of Congress Cataloging-in-Publication Data
DePaola, Tomie, 1934–
My mother is so smart / Tomie dePaola.   p. cm.
Summary: From her knowledge of when to change a diaper and how to make Popsicles to her skills in driving
a delivery truck and dancing the polka, a child sings the praises of a special family member.
[1. Mother and child–Fiction.] I. Title.   PZ7.D439Myv 2010   [E]–dc22   2009011308

ISBN 978-0-399-25442-0
1 3 5 7 9 10 8 6 4 2

I knew from the time I was really little
that my mother was smart.

She always knew when to change my diaper.

She always knew I was hungry before I cried.

When I was learning to walk, she dressed me up
in a snowsuit and let me stroll down the sidewalk
with my brother's galoshes on.

My mother is so smart,
she can make the best cookies.

And grow mint for iced tea.
And make Popsicles in the freezer.

She taught the whole neighborhood
how to sing "Row, Row, Row Your Boat."

On the Fourth of July, every kid in the neighborhood
wants to come to our yard because my mother

showed us how to be VERY careful and
make our initials in the air with sparklers.

My mother is so smart that when it's cold out,
she gives us breakfast that makes us warm.

One year, she turned me
into a bird for Halloween.

She makes our house the best house at Christmas.

My father and I help.

She knows how to drive my grandfather's
old delivery truck.

Sometimes she takes me
to school in it.

My mother is so smart, she can change into a movie star
when she and my father go out at night.

She can dance the polka,
and she taught me.

My mother is so smart that she knows just where I should be.
Once the teachers told me I had to wait outside after school.

I said, "My mother told me to wait for her right here,
and my mother knows everything."

"Well, your mother must be very smart,"
the principal said.

"She is," I answered. "My mother is so smart
that she can stand on her head."

And she can!